The Bald-Headed PRINCESS

Cancer, Chemo, and Courage

Published by
MAGINATION PRESS
An Educational Publishing Foundation Book
American Psychological Association
750 First Street, NE
Washington, DC 20002

For more information about our books, including a complete catalog, please write to us, call 1-800-374-2721, or visit our website at www.apa.org/pubs/magination.

Printed by Worzalla, Stevens Point, WI

Cover and book design by Kathy Keler
Cover photograph by Sean Russell/Getty Images

Library of Congress Cataloging-in-Publication Data
Ditmars, Maribeth R.
The bald-headed princess: cancer, chemo, and courage / by Maribeth R. Ditmars.
    p. cm.
"An Educational Publishing Foundation Book ."
Summary: With her parents by her side and new friends to tell her bad jokes, eleven-year-old "soccer princess" Izzie Salida learns to cope with her leukemia diagnosis and treatment.
  ISBN-13: 978-1-4338-0737-4 (hardcover : alk. paper)
  ISBN-10: 1-4338-0737-8 (hardcover : alk. paper)
  ISBN-13: 978-1-4338-0738-1 (pbk. : alk. paper)
  ISBN-10: 1-4338-0738-6 (pbk. : alk. paper)
[1. Cancer--Fiction. 2. Chemotherapy--Fiction. 3. Hospitals--Fiction. 4. Medical care--Fiction. 5. Jokes--Fiction. 6. Family life--Fiction.] I. Title.

PZ7.D6293Bal 2010
[Fic]--dc22   2009053263

First printing March 2010

10 9 8 7 6 5 4 3 2 1

FSC
Mixed Sources
Product group from well-managed forests, controlled sources and recycled wood or fiber
Cert no. BV-COC-080720
www.fsc.org
©1996 Forest Stewardship Council

green circle
USA
ECO-FRIENDLY BOOKS
Made in the USA

In memory of Chris Ditmars, whose favorite phrase was "don't spoil the magic," and Melissa Hammerling, who ruled in the magic land of kindergarten.

The Bald-Headed PRINCESS

Cancer, Chemo, and Courage

by Maribeth R. Ditmars

Magination Press ※ Washington, DC
American Psychological Association

Contents

Chapter 1
Soccer Princess

L et me take you back to the day that I found out I had
cancer. Yesterday. We were playing a tough team in
the summer U14 division. At 11 I am the youngest player
on my soccer team, but I got special permission to play,
being the coach's kid. It was also helpful that I could
pretty much kick everyone's butt in the U11 division. I'm
not trying to brag. Mom says I have a gift (I call it mad
skills), and I have to use it wisely (whatever that means—
it's soccer) and not get all puffed up about it. She also
says that I don't have to hide it either, which isn't a problem for me at all. I'm the fastest girl in my school, and
even though my name is Isabel "Izzie" Salida, everyone
calls me the Soccer Princess. So there I was, the Soccer
Princess, playing center midfield, which meant I had to
run a lot.

Everything should have been fine, but it really
wasn't. My chest hurt and I felt like I was moving in slow
motion. I wanted to run but I just couldn't. Everyone was
stealing the ball from me, and I felt useless. And then I
took an elbow to the face and my nose started gushing
blood. I remember feeling dizzy and hearing someone say,
"Oh no, it won't stop." Then everything went black.

When I woke up, though, that's when the real nightmare began. They put me in an ambulance and packed gauze up my nose so tight it felt like they'd shoved a brick up there. I was already crying but I blubbered even more. They poked me in the arm with a needle (I hate needles) while Mom held my hand. The gurney rattled when they unloaded me and the automatic doors whizzed open. I was in the hospital emergency room with my mom's upside-down face hovering over me. "It's okay, honey, we're here. Daddy followed the ambulance over. We'll take care of you."

But it wasn't okay. It was the longest day of my life. They made me wait for hours, and they kept sending in people with white coats to take blood out of my arm. Did I mention that I hate needles? I felt like I was being attacked by vampires. Doctors were talking to my parents behind a curtain, and then finally my parents sat down next to my bed and dropped the C-bomb: CANCER.

"We have something important to talk to you about," Dad said. His voice was strangely calm. "This is some tough news, kiddo. When the doctor tested your blood, she found out why your nose wouldn't stop bleeding at the game, why you were so tired. You have a cancer called leukemia."

That's why I had no energy at the game. CANCER. That's why the bleeding wouldn't stop. CANCER. That's why I saw my life as basically over. CANCER.

I always thought cancer was for old people. *How can someone my age get it?* I thought. I had so many questions I felt like my brain was going to explode. *Am I going to die? What about soccer? Maybe it was a mistake. Maybe they got my blood test mixed up with someone else's.* I looked back and forth at my mom and dad, waiting for them to fix it.

"Mom, Dad..." Tears burned down my cheeks. I couldn't speak.

"Princess, I know you are scared," Mom said. "Your dad and I are, too. But we're going to do everything to get you treated."

"That's right," agreed Dad. "You'll have the best medicine and the best doctors. And we'll be right by your side throughout this whole process. We're going to help you get all better."

"What?! How do you know I'm going to get better?" My heart beat faster and more tears tumbled out. "How come other kids like Lizette get to go to summer camp and I have to get CANCER and go to the hospital?! Cancer sucks! This sucks!"

"I know," agreed Mom as she got up and put her arms around me. I tried not to but I just sobbed on her shoulder. "I know, honey. I'm sorry this is happening to you. Sometimes people just get sick, and life just isn't fair. Sometimes bad things happen. Sometimes you get stuck with stuff that you never in a million years wanted."

I pushed her away. "Mom, this isn't like the time you talked me into taking ballet and wearing pink tights," I said. "This sucks-sucks-SUCKS! I don't want to be in the hospital and I don't want to miss soccer! Nothing is wrong with me. Look at me." I got out of bed and started turning around. "There must be a mistake. Really. I'm fine." I didn't believe it myself, but maybe I could convince Mom and Dad otherwise. My gauze-packed nose made my voice sound nasal and pathetic.

"Honey, you're going to be okay." Mom caressed my arm and spoke softly, but her eyes were serious. "The good news is that the doctors said leukemia is a kind of cancer that they can get rid of in kids. It's 'highly curable'," Mom said using air quotes. I hated when she used air quotes. Dad leaned over and touched my other arm.

"How long will it take?" I asked.

I had heard of leukemia, but I couldn't remember much. I remembered seeing some hospital telethon or something. Were they lying to me? How could they know my leukemia would be "highly curable" (no air quotes)? Were they just trying to humor me before I die?

What would I do in the fall when soccer season starts up? I pictured myself on the sidelines sitting in a wheelchair with no teeth, slurping up Jell-O. They'd probably give me the game ball, and they'd have this pitiful look in their eyes that people get when they feel really bad for you but have no idea what to say.

Ever since I can remember, soccer has been my life. From the time I had kicked my first soccer ball in the back yard, Dad had called me his "little soccer sensation." I learned how to dribble at three, and by four I could bounce the ball off my head. When I was six, I noticed that there was a major shortage of soccer-playing girls in my neighborhood so I begged some of the older second- and third-grade boys to let me play. At first, they all laughed at me. "Go home and play with your princess dolls!" Tommy Esposito egged me on.

"Yeah, go back to your castle, princess!" they had all yelled. Well, I don't know which made me madder—not being allowed to play or being called a princess. So I marched up to Tommy and socked him right in the nose. I'll never forget that expression on his face. His eyes teared up, and his nose bleed a little, and his mouth hung open wide enough to swallow the soccer ball whole.

"I challenge you one on one," I snarled. "First one to score five goals wins. I win, I play. You win, I go home."

Now this whole time, my best friend Lizette ("Lizzie") had been watching. And let me tell you, if anyone should be nicknamed a princess, it's definitely her. She's way more of a girlie-girl than me. She was actually wearing a princess get-up that day, which is probably what gave those boys the idea to call me a princess in the first place. I couldn't be mad at Lizette, though. I mean, she was only six at the time. And despite her girly ways, she's still my best friend, and whenever we're together we laugh a lot. We are both good artists, and we love going to the mall. When I first tried make-up, I looked like some kind of zombie clown with black eyes, but Lizzie wiped it off and did it perfectly. We definitely respect each other's differences. Even so, poor Lizzie was horrified when I popped big-mouth Tommy and then challenged him.

"Don't," Lizette moaned. "I'll play with you." But as soon as she said it, she knew it was a ridiculous thing to say.

"C'mon, Lizzie, you know you stink at soccer. Watch me. I'll show them."

By now Tommy had recovered a bit. "Okay, *Princess*, let's see what you got." He wiped the blood off of his nose, and we walked out onto the field like Harry Potter and Voldemort.

Tommy was bigger but I was faster. I swiveled my hips and slid right past him. I had scored five goals and he only had two. By the time we finished, the boys were cheering for me! Meanwhile, Lizzie had been cheering on the sidelines, and when I won, she ran up to me and proudly placed her princess tiara on my head. "Now you're the Soccer Princess!" she exclaimed. This time when everyone laughed, it was different. They weren't laughing at me. Tommy admitted that I was okay for a girl, and I decided that I was cool with being the Soccer Princess.

When Dad heard the story, he decided that I was ready to join a soccer team. "Unless, of course, you'd prefer boxing," he had said, winking at me.

And the rest, as my parents say, is history. Dad, who had always coached boys' soccer (my older cousins play, too—they're boys), started coaching my team, and Mom and Lizette became my biggest fans. Until yesterday. Now I don't know if I'll be the Soccer Princess any more.

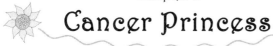

Chapter 2

Cancer Princess

So that's how I got diagnosed with sucky cancer. Overnight I went from being a soccer princess to a cancer princess. The only thing worse than getting cancer is getting cancer in the summer when your best friend is away at camp. I can't even enjoy being off from school. Lizette and I have been best friends since kindergarten, and we've never been apart for more than a week. Now when I need her most, she isn't around.

Oh, did I mention the best part about cancer? There is this delightful medicine they give you called "chemotherapy." Yesterday I thought I'd at least get to go home and pack a few things before returning to the hospital, but nooo, they decided that I have to begin my chemo right away. I am not looking forward to this. I think they stick "therapy" on the end of the word to trick patients into thinking that it's actually going to make them feel better. From what I can gather, it involves is needles, pills, and IV tubes, but I'll find out soon enough. Yippee.

If you couldn't tell, it's my first day in the hospital. Once they finally stopped my nose bleed, I got taken up in the elevator to this very floor where all the cancer patients are. Since it's a children's hospital, there are cartoons painted on the wall. *Yeah right, like a picture of*

Scooby Doo is going to make me forget I have cancer, I thought. *Maybe they can mix up a potion in cartoon-land and send it my way. Voila—cured in one half-hour episode.*

So now I sit. And wait.

While my parents are talking to the doctor in the hallway, Shania shows me to my room. She's a nurse and so far, she's pretty nice. She can tell I'm scared, and she speaks softly as she inserts a needle with a tube into my arm. "This will be over in one second," she promises. I grimace, expecting it to hurt like it had downstairs in the ER, but she really knows what she's doing. It's no worse than the pinch Tommy always gives me on St. Patrick's Day even though he's not supposed to because I always wear green.

"You were right. That wasn't bad at all." I'm starting to feel brave.

Shania smiles and explains what she's doing as I watch her connect the tube to a blue pump on the IV pole. Hanging from the top of the pole, above the pump, is a bag of clear liquid. She punches some buttons and I hear little beeping sounds. "We have to run fluids through your system first before we start your chemo." Her lipstick matches her fingernails perfectly. Lizette would approve. "I can tell you are going to be an excellent patient. And I hear that you are quite the soccer player."

"You mean *was*," I sulk.

"No, I mean *are*," Shania corrects me. "You won't have to give up soccer forever. You'll be playing again before you know it."

This is the first piece of good news I've heard all day. Yeah, my parents had told me something like this, but Shania is a medical person. She knows about cancer. This is a promise I intend to make all of the doctors and nurses keep.

After they finish speaking with the doctor, my parents sit down next to my bed. "We were talking to the oncologist, Dr. Ruckowski, and he was explaining your treatment. He'll be here in a minute to meet you."

Suddenly the word "cancer" echoes in my ears again. *Cancer. Cancer. Cancer.* And once again the you'll-play-soccer-again happiness is gone and I'm terrified... and really angry. "I don't want to meet Dr. Whats-a-kowski! I want to go home! I don't want any of this!"

"I hear you, sweetie," Mom agreed calmly. "It's a raw deal." She gives me big hug, but it doesn't help. "We talked to Dr. Ruckowski about how we will work to treat the cancer and make you better." My mom is the practical type. She is a math teacher so it comes naturally. "Do you have any questions, honey? Or would you rather rest for now?"

"What the heck *is* cancer anyway?"

"Well, the doctor said it's when one cell goes hay-wire, 'abnormal,' *(again with the air quotes!)* and starts making lots of other abnormal cells. They crowd out the good cells, and they have to be killed off with strong med-icine called chemotherapy."

"Kind of like when there's too many players on the field and no one can see the ball," Dad adds. My father, on the other hand, is the jokester in the family. He works for a big toy company. Mom always says that's because he never really grew up.

"Rafa, you'll confuse her," Mom scolds.

I don't want to but I smile for a second. Leave it to Dad to make a soccer analogy.

"How sick am I?" I wonder aloud. "Can they really make me all better? Tommy's uncle had cancer and he died."

I remember kicking the ball around with Tommy last November. After the nose job I gave him when we were six, we ended up becoming pretty good friends. Well, he was getting really frustrated when he kept messing up and he started crying. I had never seen him cry like that before. That's when he told me that his Uncle Karl was in the hospital and he was really sick with bone cancer. He was dying. I wonder if they had told his uncle in the beginning that he was going to live, too. Are they just telling me I'll get better when I'm really going to die?

"Oh honey, he had a completely different kind of cancer than you do. The chemo will work for you," Mom reassures me.

"It really will be okay, sweetie," Dad says as he rubs my back. "Your mom and I are right here. We love you very much. We're going to beat it. You're going to beat it."

"How long will it take? Will it hurt?"

Almost like he hears my questions, Dr. Ruckowski walks into the room. He's friendly and tall with shaggy brown hair, and his glasses wiggle on his nose when he smiles. "Well, this must be the famous Soccer Princess." He reaches out his hand to shake mine. I try to smile, feeling a little embarrassed, but I like him. He looks me in the eye and doesn't talk to me like I'm some stupid little kid.

He explains that I'll have to be in and out of the hospital for about eight months. Eight months! After that, I only have to visit the outpatient clinic once a week. I'll miss school, but they have a teacher at the hospital and they can send a tutor to our house when I'm at home. Soccer will have to wait for a while.

"When we are all done, your cancer will be gone," Dr. Ruckowski concludes.

I barely hear that last part. All I can think of is how much everything is going to change. No school. No soccer. No friends?!

I try not to think about it. But my mind drifts to the time that Lizzie and I laid in the grass on a warm spring day and wished we never had to go to school. We talked about all the drawing and skating we could do all day. How am I supposed to feel now that I can't even go to school? I feel like I'm going to be stuck in here forever.

"Be careful what you wish for," my mom always says. I guess this is what she means.

Lizzie and I were supposed to be in the same class this year, and I'm supposed to play on a championship team. Lizzie and I are supposed to go shopping as soon as she gets home from camp. And what about the Labor Day cookout? Dad and I have been planning that forever. We always set up soccer and softball for the older kids, and badminton and kiddie pools for the younger kids. Now it sounds like I'm not even allowed to go to that. Now I live in the hospital. Now I have cancer. Now I don't get to do anything. My parents are talking to me, but I'm not listening anymore. I curl up under the covers and cry myself to sleep.

Chapter 3
Hospital Princess

I wake up a lot during the night. Every single time I think I'm at home, and I want to cry as soon as I realize where I am. I was dreaming that I was riding on a float in a parade after my soccer team had won the world championship, but then the float started making this loud beeping sound and the crowd suddenly disappeared. When I open my eyes, the pump on my IV pole is beeping. Why can't this part be the dream?

I see my mom stretched out on a pull-out next to my bed. "Mom, I'm beeping! Help!"

Just then, a light stabs my eyes as the door opens and someone comes in. "Hi, I'm Freddy, your night nurse. Don't worry about the beeping. That just tells us we need to reset your pump." I just stare at Freddy. "Hey," he says perkily, "it's almost morning, and you're going to get a roommate who's about the same age as you."

Freddy is tall and skinny with a really short buzz cut. He looks more like a basketball player than a nurse. And he is way too cheerful for the wee hours of the morning if you ask me.

By now my mom is sitting up, and the two of them are talking about how they gave me a unit of blood during the night. I glance up and saw a reddish bag hanging from my pole, but I'm more curious about my new roommate. Another kid with cancer—well, at least I'm not alone in this loony bin.

After a couple of more hours of just tossing and turning in bed, it is morning and Shania returns.

"Here is someone I'd like you to meet. This is Natalie. She's a cancer patient, too, and she'll be your room-mate while you are here. She can show you all around."

Except for her really short hair, Natalie looks like a regular girl, not someone with cancer. She looks a little older than me and she has a drawing pad. Cool, she likes to draw, too. I'm so relieved that I'm not getting some kind of a freak for a roommate.

Shania introduces Natalie's mom, Mrs. Cornelli, and she and my mom seem to hit it off instantly. It is so incredibly strange. I'm used to soccer-mom talk on the sidelines, not cancer-mom talk.

"So what are you in for?" Natalie smiles as she puts her things down. "I have Ewing's Sarcoma."

My heart starts pounding. "I...I have leukemia," I stammer. I am completely weirded out having to say it for the first time. I'm not even sure if I really believe it. My eyes tear up. I fight the urge to break down.

Natalie sees me squirming and almost crying. "It's okay. We don't have to talk now. C'mon, I'll show you around."

"Go ahead, dear." Mom seems happy that I have a new friend.

Natalie shows me how to unplug the power cord

attached to my IV pole and attach it to a strap that snaps onto to the pole. "Now you're ready to roll." As we step out into the hallway, Natalie points to the wheels at the bottom of the pole. "These things make awesome scooters. We're not supposed to ride them, but everybody does."

So I climb on and push off. It is so much fun gliding down the hall! Hospital staff walk by and smile at us. "This is Isabel. She's new," Natalie explains to everyone. First she shows me the playroom at the end of the hall. It has tables, a bumper pool table, video games, shelves of books, a toy kitchen set, lots of cushions, and a big-screen TV. I see a small girl sitting at one of the tables with an adult working on one of those big wooden puzzles. There is a little bald toddler in a toy car pushing his way across the room making "VROOOOOM" sounds. His mother is chasing after him, pushing his IV pole. He stops when he sees us and waves. His poor mom almost trips over his car. "Hi, Nah Nah."

"Hi, Josh," Natalie waves back. "This is Isabel."

"Izzzbel."

We all laugh. "You can call me Izzie," I say.

"Izzie."

"Do all the kids here have cancer, too?" I ask Natalie.

"Yup, it's an oncology floor," she answers matter-of-factly. Seeing kids acting normal makes me feel a little better. They don't even act like they have cancer. At least I won't have to spend all of my time in bed with tubes and electrodes attached to me. That was what I had been imagining last night. Glad that's not the case.

As we go back out into the hall, Natalie spots Shania at the other end of the corridor. "Quick, let's get on the elevator before she sees me. She's looking for me so she can hook up my IV. Get on." I hop onto my pole.

Natalie grabs my pole and races me towards the elevator. I laugh out loud as we fly past a cart full of trays, narrowly missing it. I like this Natalie girl. She is a rebel, a real troublemaker like me. I wonder if she plays soccer. "Hurry up, stupid elevator!" she yells, laughing. Just as the doors whiz open, Shania sees us.

"Natalie Rose Cornelli, get your little self over here!" Shania calls out. "You know you..." Too late—we are going up.

"Where are we going?" I gasp, out of breath with excitement.

"I'm giving you the grand tour before the cancer police catch us."

Natalie takes me up to the rooftop playground, complete with a basketball hoop and a decent view of the city below. Then we ride all the way down to the cafeteria on the bottom floor. I suddenly realize that I am still in my pajamas and slippers. Then just as quickly, I remember this is a hospital and just about everyone is in pjs and gowns. Not exactly fashion central. Lizzie would hate it. Sure enough, no one seems to notice as Natalie leads me up to the counter. "Hi, Miss Margaret," Natalie greets an older lady with a hair net who is standing right by the orange Jell-O cups. By the way, why do hospitals always have orange Jell-O? They aren't going to make me eat anything that jiggles.

"Well, hello, Natalie. Who do we have here?" Miss Margaret's eyes twinkle behind her wire-frame glasses.

"I'm so glad you asked," Natalie grinned. "This is Isabel. And were you aware of the new hospital policy regarding free cookies for all new patients and their friends?"

"You don't say?" Miss Margaret folds her arms across her chest but keeps smiling. "Was that rule made by the same folks who made the double pudding for all the Ewing's Sarcoma patients rule? As I recall, that policy was created the last time you were here."

"Well, what a coincidence!" Natalie chirps. "But rules are rules." She holds out her hand and nudges me to do the same. This girl is good. She could probably talk them into installing a swimming pool in the parking lot.

Miss Margaret produces two chocolate chip cookies. They are warm and gooey. "Now go on. Get out of here before you get me in trouble."

As we ride the elevator back to our floor, I realize that Natalie had almost made me forget that I had cancer. Almost.

As we scoot back to our room, Natalie smiles at me and says, "The first day in the hospital is always the best. They haven't had a chance to make you sick yet."

Chapter 4

Surgery Princess

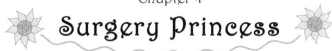

When we get back to the room, Dad is there. "There's my princess! Have they put you in charge yet?" He hugs me just a little too hard and it makes my arm hurt where my IV is.

"Ouch! No, Dad, they don't have team captains on an oncology floor." I roll my eyes.

"Well, listen to you. You sound like a doctor!" Dad smiles and then takes out a stuffed soccer ball and head-bumps it towards me, yelling, "Think fast!" Dad could be sooo embarrassing. I ignore the ball and it lands on the bed. I rub my arm where the IV is.

"Dad, this is Natalie. She showed me all around."

"Hey, sport, a pleasure to make your acquaintance." He reaches out his hand and gives Natalie a high-five. Oh please, we're not at sports camp, Dad. Give it a rest.

"Nice to meet you," Natalie giggles.

"Where's Mom?" I'm desperate for a sane adult.

"She just went to get coffee. She'll be right back."

Just then, Shania comes in with a bag of weird looking liquid and some tubing in one hand and her other hand on her hip. She tries to glare at Natalie, but her eyes are smiling. "Girl, you just better sit yourself down on that bed before I tie you down!"

I watch as Natalie lifts up her shirt and exposes a little tube that hangs out of a bandage on her chest. That is weird. You try not staring a tube coming out of someone's chest. It's nearly impossible. Anyway, Shania attaches her IV to the tube instead of inserting a needle in her arm. That must be some strange kind of cancer she's got.

I think about asking Natalie why she has a tube in her chest, but I don't want to be rude. Before I can decide what to say, Mom walks in with yet another woman. Seriously! How many people are going to meet with me?

"Hi, Isabel. I'm Alexis and I am a child life specialist. I'm here to answer any questions you have and generally explain things. I want to make your stay here as comfortable as possible. If there are any games, books, or movies you like I can try to get them for you."

"Oh, okay."

"How are you feeling? A little overwhelmed? It's a little scary, isn't it?"

"Actually, it's a lot scary," I reply. "How do people get cancer anyway?"

"We know the causes of some cancers. For example, we know that smoking causes lung cancer, but nobody really knows what causes leukemia. It starts with one mutated white blood cell that goes haywire."

"So, the chemo keeps it from taking over my body?"

"Exactly. As a matter of a fact, I wanted to talk to you and your parents about what to expect in the next few days. Dr. Ruckowski said you're going to get a mediport put in, and then you'll start your chemotherapy."

"What's a mediport?" I looked at my parents, but they just made those cutesy little everything's-going-to-be-alright-honey smiles. They used those same smiles when I was really sick one time and had to get a gigantic needle in my butt. I hate those smiles.

Alexis pulls a doll out of a bag by her chair. What, we're going to play hospital now? Lady, I'm eleven going on twelve, not three.

Alexis reads my mind. "Don't worry. I'm not going to make you play with dolls. This is Ralphie and he has a mediport. I just wanted you to see what it looks like. See, it's a little device that goes in your chest just under the skin, and it connects to your veins under there so the nurses don't have to stick you all the time."

When I see the tube coming out of the doll's chest, I say, "That's what Natalie has." Little Vroom-Vroom Josh must have had a mediport, too, because his arms were free.

By now Shania has left, and Natalie is listening from her bed. "It's really nice having a port. They just plug in your chemo. It doesn't even hurt."

"So *everyone* has to get one of those things?" My vision with the tubes and electrodes is back. "How do they put it in there?"

"It's minor surgery," Alexis says. "It's quick and you won't feel a thing."

Surgery?! First cancer, then chemo. Now surgery! I hang my head as Mom squeezes my hand. "We'll be there in the surgery room with you, and we'll be there when you wake up," she promises.

"This really sucks. Do I have to do it?" I know that is a stupid question as soon as I ask it.

"We have flavored anesthesia. You can get root beer, cherry, lemonade, and more." Alexis is trying to cheer me up, but it isn't working.

"Oh goody, goody." I fold my arms across my chest. "Do I get to pick the color of the scalpel, too?" I have never had surgery before, but I've seen plenty of doctor movies so I know things. My eyes are angry but my heart is scared.

Alexis opens her mouth to say something, but Natalie interrupts. "Look at that stupid IV in your arm. After a couple of days, it gets all puffy and bruised. Trust me. You want to ditch it."

Well, it did hurt when Dad bumped it. "Okay," I sigh. "When?"

"Tomorrow," Alexis answers. "And like Natalie said, you'll be a lot more comfortable with the IV out of your arm. It'll be over before you know it."

Chapter 5
Chemo Princess

Well, I hate to admit it. They were right. I chose cherry and it was a piece of cake. I guess sometimes the fear of something is a lot worse than the something itself.

I hope the same is true for the chemo. I have a feeling it isn't.

When I get back to the room, Natalie calls me an official cancer kid. Oh goody. They can x-ray me and see a port inside. It reminds me of an alien movie that I saw once. The aliens looked like regular humans except when they x-rayed them, there was this microchip inside of them. The chip gave them superhuman powers. Now I am different, too. There is no turning back. If only my port were an alien chip that could instantly zap away the cancer.

A little later, I'm playing cards with Mom, but not really paying attention because of all of the stuff in my head, when Dr. Ruckowski comes in to check the bandage where I had my surgery.

"Looks good," he smiles. "How are you feeling?"

"Okay." I am still a little tired but I'm nervous, too. What now?

"The surgery went very well," the doctor continues. "With your port in, we don't have to stick your veins anymore. You can start your chemo now."

Well, he answered that question, didn't he?

"Do you have any questions?"

"Yes, I have a question," Mom says. "Exactly how does the chemo work to kill the cancer cells?"

"Well, like we discussed, cancer cells divide and reproduce very rapidly, faster than normal cells. Left unchecked, they will kill off all of the healthy cells. Chemotherapy is very strong medicine that is designed to target the fast growing cancer cells. Unfortunately, it does have some side effects."

"Side effects?" I glance nervously at Mom. She starts rubbing my back, but I push her away.

"Yes," the doctor continues, "chemo kills some of the healthy cells, too, and that might make you feel sick."

"How sick?" I do not like the sound of this. My heart starts beating faster and it makes my chest throb where they put in my port.

"Well, that really varies from patient to patient, but most of our kids don't have a lot of serious side effects. We also can give you anti-nausea medicine that helps a lot."

Peachy. First they are going to give me medicine that makes me sick, then they are going to give me more medicine to make me unsick. It all sounds pretty sick to me.

"There is one more side effect I have to tell you about." Dr. Ruckowski hesitates. I can tell that he has probably explained this stuff a million times before but he still hates doing it. "You will most likely experience hair loss."

I shoot a panicked look at my mom. Tell me it isn't true! Even Mom has tears in her eyes.

Now, I have to explain here that I have a lot of hair. It's long and thick, and when I play soccer, I put it up in a pony tail with a hair tie that has little soccer balls on it. My hair has always been the one thing that has kept me from being a total tomboy. One time when some of the girls made fun of me for playing sports with the guys, I shut them up by pulling out my hair tie and letting my hair down. "You're just jealous of the Soccer Princess!" I told them. Then I spun on my heels and flicked it back behind my shoulders like the models in the shampoo commercials. Lizette and I love to style each others' hair. I absolutely can not imagine myself without hair.

"You mean I'm going to go BALD!" I practically scream. For a second I feel sorry for yelling at Dr. R. Then I burst into tears.

Mom starts rubbing my back again and this time I let her. "How long until that happens?" she asks.

"Usually a few weeks after the chemo starts, but that varies, too. Some patients don't lose their hair, but most do. I can promise you one thing though—it always grows back when your chemo is done."

"Well, I'm not going to lose my hair!" I frown defiantly. "I won't. Mom, you'll see."

"You tell them," Natalie cheers. "Try to will your hair follicles into submission."

Mom smiles at Natalie and looks at me seriously. "Well, if you do lose your hair, remember it always grows back," Mom says softly. "And you'll always be our beautiful Soccer Princess."

"Hey," Natalie gets my attention. "Don't mourn hair that hasn't even been lost yet. Who knows, maybe your ends won't split after all."

I just look at her, and it takes me a second to get her joke. Before I can say anything, Shania comes in with the dreaded bag of chemo. Right before she hangs the bag on my pole, she puts on this ridiculous looking plastic blue gown, complete with gloves and a hat.

"You look attractive," I mutter.

"Well, thank you honey. I was thinking about buying the matching purse the next time I'm at Saks." Mom and I smile in spite of the situation.

The chemo is a weird yellow color. "It looks like a big bag of pee," I announce trying to get a rise out of her.

"Yup, sure enough does. We all call it Gatorade," Shania responds, winking. "Now, you just push your call button if you need anything." Natalie was right. I am now an official cancer kid with a port and a big 'ole bag of Gatorade at my side.

The rest of the afternoon goes okay considering. Natalie and I hang out in the playroom for a while and entertain Vroom-Vroom Josh with a Nerf ball. He is too young to catch it, but he loves trying. We all laugh as it bounces off his little bald head. Is that what my head is going to look like? I glance around at some of the other kids in the room. Some have hair and some wear hats. One little girl has thin wisps on her head that remind me of my Papi's hair.

"Natalie, did you lose your hair?"

"Yeah, I had long hair like you, but when it started falling out, I got it cut short. Now it's grown back a little, but they said it might come out again after this cycle of chemo." She just shrugs and tosses the ball over Josh's head to a little girl named Ayana who hands it to back to him. Jeez, she may as well be chatting about what she had for breakfast. We're talking hair here.

"Didn't it bother you?"

"Sure, but as Alexis says, it's a small price to pay to have your life saved. Hey," she says changing the subject, "There's a teen movie night in here tonight. Alexis says we're old enough. Want to go?"

"Okay."

Right about the time the movie is supposed to start, Dad comes by. He had stopped at Wendy's after work to get my favorite burger. He and Mom start spreading the food out on my tray when I smell this awful smell. It stabs my nostrils and makes my stomach churn. Gross, it stinks like hot, wet garbage. I suddenly realize it's the food. "Ewwww, get it out of here," I groan. "It's making me sick!"

Mom and Dad scramble to scoop up the food. I can feel my stomach tighten.

"Quick! Get me a bucket!"

Too late. I lean over and vomit on the floor. I can feel the sweat on my forehead, and I can hear my puke splat onto the tile. Then the smell of the puke makes my stomach leap, but there was nothing left to throw up. Well, I'll never make it to the movie.

Dad runs out into the hall to get help as I curl up in bed gasping. Mom tries to comfort me, but I don't want anyone touch me. Finally, they give me some anti-nausea medicine in my IV, and after a few more minutes of agony, it starts working. My stomach feels better, but my brain is spinning. So this is chemo. I get to throw up and go bald. When Lizzie gets back from camp, she probably won't want to hang out with me.

Chapter 6
Friendship Princess

The next morning I'm feeling somewhat human. Every few hours they give me medicine for nausea. Natalie tells me that I'll still get sick sometimes, but it won't last all day. "It's kind of like having the flu in spurts," she explains. "One time I was eating a slice of pizza, I threw up, then 10 minutes later I ate three more slices. So when you're feeling okay you have to go for it. And if you puke, so what? You're already in the hospital. Milk it for as much as you can. Get them to bring you movies and stuff."

I laugh. I knew I liked this girl. It's weird. I'm feeling closer to Natalie than I do to Lizette. Natalie knows what I am going through. Lizette, well, she's clueless. It's almost like I suddenly had to grow up and Lizette is still a little kid.

Then, as if she's reading my mind, Mom comes in the door. "Hey, guess what?! You got a postcard from Lizzie." She hands me a postcard with a picture of a lake set in the mountains. On the back is Lizzie's familiar loopy handwriting. She has written about canoeing and horse-back riding. There is no mention of me being sick.

"She doesn't even know, does she?" I'm suddenly angry.

"Oh honey, the camp is pretty far away and phone

calls are limited. Her mom probably hasn't had a chance to tell her."

Yeah, right. She just doesn't care. She's too busy galloping through the woods, making new friends. "Mom, this so sucks!" I fling the postcard across the hospital room. It hits the wall and ricochets onto the floor. Mom wisely doesn't try to pick it up.

"Sweetheart—"

"Mom, don't even go there! Why don't you just go get coffee or something?!" I bury myself under the covers. Lizette's learning how to jump logs on horseback, and I'm learning about the side effects of chemotherapy. I'm not sure how long I stay under there, and I think Natalie tries to cheer me up, but I just ignore her. I feel bad ignoring her, but I can't help it. It's like the time when I was six and my Labrador, Newton, got run over by a car. He was suddenly gone forever. I didn't want to talk about it for a while. Now it seems like soccer is gone, my best friend is gone, my life is gone.

Finally, I have to come out of my cave of covers to meet another counselor. "Hi, Isabel, I'm Chris. I work with Alexis. I heard you were having a rough day." I lower the covers just enough to peek at him. Well, he is kind of cute. He's blonde and has a bunch of freckles on his nose. He looks athletic.

"Yeah," I mumble.

"Did you know that I'm a leukemia survivor?"

"Really?" I lower the covers a little more.

"Yeah, I was about your age. I was playing soccer and running track. My times started getting slower, and I started getting weird bruises. When they took me to the doctor, he did some tests and they told me I had leukemia. I had never even heard of it. I had to be in and out of the hospital for a year and it was the pits. But now I'm fine. I've been in remission for 17 years now. That's what made me decide to work with sick kids."

"I play soccer, you know," I perk up.

"Awesome!" Chris's face lights up. "I have a ball. Let's go kick it around on the rooftop playground."

"We're allowed?"

"I have never seen a sign up there that says 'no soccer playing'."

"I bet there isn't one that says 'no throwing water balloons off the roof' either!"

"Ahh, you're my kind of patient." Chris's eyes twinkle. "I can see that we're going to have some fun together."

We ride the elevator up, and Chris twirls the soccer ball on his finger like a basketball. He tells me how he was able to go back to sports when his treatment was over. By the time he graduated high school, only a few people even knew what he had been through. "I made varsity in my sophomore year, and I even got a partial scholarship in college. In the long run, I think fighting cancer made me a stronger person. And once it was behind me, I really appreciated being healthy again and I didn't sweat the small stuff."

"Well, I'd rather not have cancer and not be quite as good a person," I joke.

Chris laughs. "So you'd rather be a healthy brat."

"Exactly."

It's interesting trying to kick a soccer ball while toting my trusty pole and my Gatorade. I can't really run, but I can use my pole to block balls that I can't reach with my feet. Before we know it, the other kids up there join in. We're all giggling and shuffling around like a bunch of old people with walkers who suddenly turn young again.

"You got some moves, kid. I can tell you're really good."

I don't have enough energy to last more than a few minutes, but it still feels great. We sit down at a picnic table, and I end up telling Chris all about Lizette and how I got my nickname.

"Chris, did your friends stick by you when you were sick?"

"My good ones did. Some kids laughed at me when I was bald, but they weren't my real friends anyway."

"What did you do?"

"I just tried to ignore them. I had a lot of other people around me who cared. They more than made up for it."

"Did it make you mad when they were healthy and you were stuck in the hospital?"

"Oh yeah. Especially when this girl I liked went to the seventh grade dance with Marty Schwartz. I wanted to punch out Marty Schwartz."

"Yeah, me too!"

"You know Marty Schwartz?" Chris teases me. "He'd be a little old for you."

"No, no," I giggle. "I mean I want to slap Lizette. You know, for being at camp and all while I'm here." But as soon as I say it, I don't want to do it anymore. Saying the words out loud makes my anger inside fizzle out. I feel a lot better, at least until I start feeling sick again.

I have to go back to bed. I feel achy, but at least I'm not nauseous. I think about Lizzie and our secret hideout. There is this old church a few blocks from our street, and we love climbing up in the bell tower. At first Lizzie was scared, but I double-dared her up the narrow stairs. The cobwebs freaked her out a little, so I told her they were dead webs that the spiders had long since abandoned. We started bringing blankets and stuff up there and stashing them. Pretty soon it felt like we owned it. Except for a few pigeons that we eventually named, it was completely private. We would bring up our sketch pads and Barbie dolls and spend hours up there. We called it our Castle Club.

I smile whenever I think of the time we almost got caught when someone rang the bell and Lizzie screamed. I started making caw sounds like a crow so they would think her scream was just a dumb bird. But it worked and no one bothered us, except there was some sort of ceremony going on in the chapel, and we had to wait until they were done to sneak out of there. We both had to go to the bathroom, too, and we started giggling and shushing each other.

I start laughing out loud, but then I remember where I am. I feel so weak now I doubt that I could even make it up those stairs. I wonder if Lizette will end up sharing our hideout with someone else. I try to focus on what Chris said. Your good friends will stick by you.

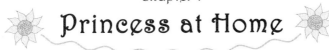 Princess at Home

Finally, I get to go home. It took a few days to finish my chemo infusions, and then they had to flush my system with IV fluids. I feel a little bit like a toilet. Poison in, flush, poison out. I hope they're flushing out all of the cancer, too. Another nurse named Tricia comes by to explain my treatment schedule. I have to come back to the hospital twice a month and visit the clinic once a week when I'm at home. In between, there will be tons of pills and medicine. The hospitalizations are going to last for eight months! I'm going to be a busy little toilet.

"I know I'm going to miss a lot of school, but can I go if I feel okay?" I ask Tricia.

"I'm afraid not, dear. The chemo is going to make your immune system very weak. You're going to have to stay away from germs and crowded places."

One more cancer side effect—no school! I am supposed to start sixth grade in a few weeks. I can see it now. My class all sitting at their desks except for one empty desk with a laptop sitting on top of it. I'm in bed with my webcam, staring pathetically out of the screen at them. Lizette walks by without noticing. She's too busy with all of her new friends. I have been reduced to a picture on the screen.

When I get home, I'm wiped out. I think even my exhaustion is tired. Mom says that the chemo will make my blood counts continue to drop, and then they will slowly come back up again. Now I know what it must feel like to be old. My bones ache, and it takes all the energy I can muster to get up and play a board game with Mom and Dad.

"How about Trivial Pursuit?" Dad asks in his Mr. Cheerful Coach voice.

"Did you wipe the pieces off with sanitizer?" Mom asks as Dad is setting up.

"Relax, dear. None of the little fellows have been sick lately." Dad picks up a little green playing piece and quizzes it. "Have you had all of your shots, Mr. Greenie?"

"Yeah," I chime in. "He looks healthy, but I don't know about Mr. Blue over there. I thought I heard him cough. Quick, Dad, toss him back in the box before he infects the others!"

Mom tries not to smile, and I giggle while Dad makes a big show of wrestling a reluctant Mr. Blue back into the box. "No, no, I want to play!" He makes a ridiculous high voice. Dad can always make me laugh.

So, I forget about how tired I am for a little while and concentrate on the game. When I start yawning, Mom puts her arm around my shoulder. "I'm so proud of you, honey. You are incredibly brave. I know you'll go into remission. Just keep up your positive attitude. That will help you get better faster."

"Do you really think so?"

"Absolutely. Attitude is everything. Keep thinking positive thoughts, and your body will heal faster. Of course, it's still okay to cry and get mad sometimes. Everyone's human."

The next few days, as my counts drop, I try to focus on what Mom had said about a positive, healing attitude. I imagine my brain cells ordering my cancer cells to die. I picture a raging battle inside my veins as tiny slimy green cancer creatures are being stabbed to death by the little caped chemo heroes. I draw the scene in my sketch pad and leave it on my nightstand to inspire me as the side effects kick in.

When the worst day comes, I can't even get out of bed at all. The inside of my mouth is filled with sores that make it hurt to eat. Everyone knows how much one little cold sore hurts. Now imagine having them all over your lips and inside your mouth. Today I remember the rest of Mom's advice—it is still okay to cry.

The phone and the doorbell ring a lot my first week home. I'm too sick to see anyone, but Mom tells me about my well-wishers.

"Your soccer team is bringing over dinners, and Aunt Lucia made your favorite dessert and—"

"Mom, I can't even eat," I mutter. "And if I did, I'd just throw it all up. All they're going to do is just make my puke more colorful."

"Aw, my poor princess." Mom brushes the hair off my forehead. "You still manage to keep your sense of humor even when you're so sick. I love you. And all of those people bringing food, they love you, too. That's how they're showing it. Hang in there. Your counts will start recovering in a day or so."

Several days later, I do feel better. I have my blood counts checked at the clinic and they say I can have visitors or go out. "Why don't we invite your cousin Nina over and go see a matinee?" Mom suggests. "The matinee won't be that crowded." There's germ phobic Mom again. She'll probably tell the manager to sanitize all of the seats, too.

"I wish Lizzie were back from camp," I sigh. Mom and her sister Lucia are pretty close, which means I get to spend lots of time with my cousin Nina and her annoying little brother Ricky. Nina is a year younger than me and she's cool, but Ricky is six going on two. He is a total pest, and Mom and Aunt Lucia are always asking us to watch him.

"Does Ricky have to come?" I moan.

"Don't worry, we'll make him sit with us so you girls can be alone." Ahh, a Ricky break. Maybe I can milk this cancer bit for all it's worth.

When they come over, Aunt Lucia grabs my cheeks and squeezes so hard I think my mouth sores are going to come back. "Ay pobre princesa, are you feeling okay?"

"Yeah, I'm fine." Suddenly, I feel embarrassed. Oh geeze, now I have to face all of these relatives who are going to feel sorry for me. What do I say?

Nina doesn't say anything about my being sick. Aunt Lucia must have told her not to ask, but apparently

Ricky missed that memo. He sticks out his tongue and blows a big raspberry. "Izzie's got cooties! Izzie's got cooties! Izzie's got…"

Before I can say anything (or strangle him), Aunt Lucia takes Ricky into another room. I hear her yelling, and then a door slams shut. Nina and I giggle while Ricky receives his attitude adjustment.

"No problema," I say when Aunt Lucia comes out to apologize. "Mom said Nina and I could sit by ourselves." At least now they won't even try to ask us to watch him.

I feel like a normal kid again while Nina and I sit several rows behind them in the dark and pelt the back of Ricky's fat little neck with gumdrops. When the gumdrops run out we make miniature Frisbees out of SweeTarts. We giggle when Aunt Nina shushes him for whining. They wouldn't kick a kid who had cancer out of the movies. This is awesome! I don't even care what the movie is about. Take that you little booger!

I realize that what Mom had said was true. It hasn't taken long for me to feel like my old self again. But she left out the part about how as soon as you feel normal again, it's time to go back in for more treatment.

Chapter 8

Bald-Headed Princess

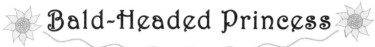

So I'm back to the hospital for a regular chemo treatment. This time I'm not so scared. Now I know the names of most of the doctors and nurses and some of the patients. Because this is an oncology floor, lots of the same kids have to keep coming back also. It's almost like a neighborhood. But it's a very dangerous one. Instead of gangs and bullets, there's the big C lurking around the corner.

Natalie isn't there when I come in. This time I have a different roommate, a younger girl who looks like she's in kindergarten. She doesn't have a hair on her head. I try to be friendly, but I am really disappointed that Natalie isn't here. "Hi," I say less than enthusiastically.

"Hi, I'm Vanessa. What's your name? Do you like to color? I have a Dora coloring book, and I have one with Sponge Bob, too. You can share one if you like. Do you have cancer, too? My mom says I'm getting all better."

Oh lovely, a roommate who's a blabbermouth. Okay, Izzie, be nice.

"I'm Isabel. Nice to meet you. No thanks on the coloring book. I prefer drawing."

"Oh, maybe Izzie can teach you to draw!" Mom says.

Sure, Mom, you get to leave whenever you want.

"Oh, you can draw?!" Vanessa puts down her coloring book. "So can my Uncle Dave. He can draw anything. He draws ponies for me. Can you draw ponies? Will you draw me a pony, please?"

Where is my iPod? I hope I remembered my headphones. "Uh, sure."

So I amuse little Vanessa Babble-on with my drawings for a while. She keeps asking me to draw different things. After sketching the usual ponies and princesses, I tell her it's my turn to pick and I draw a funny hospital scene. I draw a cartoon of Shania with a giant bag of chemo. Dr. R is standing next to her with an enormous needle in his hand, and scared little cancer cells are running across the bottom of the picture. We hang it on the bulletin board, and the rest of the day Vanessa shows it to everyone who walks by and announces, "Isabel drew that for me!" She even tries to get Vroom-Vroom Josh to come in and look at it, but he won't get out of his car.

Later, Vanessa drags me to the playroom to play house in the toy kitchen. "All right," I tell her, "But I get to be the rock-star mom with her own reality show." I have to admit that by the end of the day the little motor-mouth has me charmed. I wonder if I will get to be a mom someday. I gotta beat this cancer first.

The next day the chemo has me dragging so I just hang out in bed. I'm all sweaty and clammy so I decide to put my hair up in a pony tail. That's when it starts. My worst nightmare. My brush is filled with huge chunks of hair! I touch the top of my head and when I take my hand away, there is more hair between my fingers. I gasp. No, not me! Then I see clumps of hair on my pillow.

"Mom, Mom, make it stop!" I sob as Mom comes over to the bed and sees the hair in my hand. "Oh sweetheart, I'm so sorry. But remember what Dr. R said. It's only temporary. It always grows back prettier than ever."

"Leave me alone!" I dive under the covers. I'm ugly. Ugly and gross! I'm staying under the covers forever! Cancer took soccer, school, my best friend, and now it's stealing my hair! I cry myself to sleep.

When I wake up, it's dark and my IV pump is beeping. Freddy comes in quietly. "Oh, you're awake. You know, I hear there's a lot of baldness going around here. It must be contagious."

"You're not funny," I growl.

"If you want, we can cut it short for you. At least Shania can. I'd do it, but you'd end up looking like you got run over by a lawn mower."

"You're still not funny."

The kids all like Freddy because he is always good for a laugh. But he is totally annoying me right now.

"You think it's funny because you're a boy. It's awful when a girl goes bald."

"Isabel, I didn't mean to hurt your feelings. I think sometimes when we're faced with a situation we can't change, the best treatment is laughter."

"But I'm not even bald yet. I'm not ready to laugh!" I cross my arms across my chest.

"I'm sorry. Why don't you try to get some sleep?"

When I finally fall back asleep, I dream that I am Rapunzel, that fairy tale princess that gets locked up in the tower and lowers her hair down so the prince can climb up and rescue her. In my dream the prince is my dad, but just before he gets to me, all my hair falls out and I watch him fall into a moat full of alligators.

In the morning when Shania comes in, she acts like she doesn't notice that I have been shedding hair all night. I feel like a dog.

"Well, we have ourselves some little artist here." She nods at my drawing by Vanessa's bed. Vanessa is still asleep so we are babble-free for the time being. "Whatcha doing drawing my hips that big?"

"Well, it is a cartoon," I say, blushing.

"Mmmm hmmm." She folds her arms and raises her eyebrows. I notice that her pink eye shadow matches her scrubs. "Now, Dr. R, you got him down pat, shaggy hair and all." Funny how people always think cartoons of other people are more accurate.

Finally, Shania turns her attention to the hair all over my pillowcase.

"Why don't you let me trim that for you, honey? It'll make it a lot easier."

While I'm sitting there thinking about her offer, I hear a familiar voice down the hall.

"Now, Ricky, you behave o no helado." It was the unmistakable voice of Aunt Lucia. Oh no, my noisy family! They've all come to watch my hair fall out. And why does Aunt Lucia always have to bring Ricky? Does she honestly think he'll behave better if she bribes him? This kid is a brat in any language.

I give Mom my best make-them-go-away look, but it's too late. I am about to be totally embarrassed. Quickly, I brush the hair on my pillow onto the floor at the far side of my bed. Maybe they won't notice.

When they enter, Vanessa wakes up and immediately starts asking questions. It is a relief not to have to talk. I giggle when she asks Ricky if he has cancer, too. Then I see Nina and Aunt Lucia give Ricky a weird look. "Don't you have something to say to Isabel, Ricky?"

Ricky looks at his feet. "Izzie, I'm sorry I said you had cooties. Mama says I shouldn't have..."

I'm twirling a strand of hair in my fingers, a habit of mine. The strand comes out so easily that I don't feel a thing. Suddenly, I have an evil thought. I turn and wink at Vanessa and mouth, "Watch this."

"You know, Ricky, what you said really upset me. Why, it made me just want to tear my hair out." I make a face like I am really angry and in a lot of pain and rip out a huge wad of hair! Ricky's eyes are the size of golf balls and his mouth hangs open in horror. "It made me mad!" I pull out another chunk and fling it dramatically towards my family.

Before the hair hits the floor, Ricky darts out the door and goes screaming down the hallway. I hear a thump as he bumps into Vroom-Vroom Josh's car and a crash when someone drops a tray. I laugh so hard tears are streaming down my cheeks. When Nina and Vanessa get over their shock, they start laughing, too. The adults just stand there. I think they are deciding whether they should laugh or cry. Mom starts laughing a little. Aunt Lucia lets a giggle slip, saying, "You're bad, mala princesa," and runs after Ricky. I think this will probably be the only time Aunt Lucia will bring Ricky to the hospital to visit.

I can't wait to tell Freddy and Natalie all about it.

Chapter 9

Texting Princess

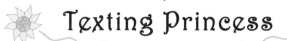

After another night of shedding, I take Freddie's advice and ask Shania to cut it short. "Well, honey, why don't you just go down to the front lobby and yank it all out and watch all the folks run out the door?" Shania teases. It seems like everyone has heard about my joke on Ricky. She tries to act like she is mad at me, but I can tell she admires the creativity of my prank.

"Oh, could I?"

"Oh, hush, or you're gonna get a really bad haircut."

A bad haircut? Why not an awesome one? "Can I have a Mohawk?" Why should I just roll over and go bald like all the other patients?

Mom looks at me like I'm nuts. "A Mohawk?" Dad smiles and gives me a sly thumbs-up.

"C'mon, Mom. I may as well go bald with style." I had originally planned to indulge myself in a major princess pout after my haircut, but this is much more fun.

Mom smiles and nods. Shania grins. "You're a piece of work, girl. Let me get the clippers." She shaves my hair at the sides and leaves one spike on top. I feel like a warrior in the battle against cancer. The Great Warrior Princess!

I just know my new look is worth a couple of free

cookies from Miss Margaret in the cafeteria. "C'mon, Vanessa, let's go down to the cafeteria." So instead of pouting about losing my hair, I get dessert. Yeah, look at me. I have cancer. Got a problem with that?

"Wow, I wish I had some hair left so I could do that!" Vanessa is in awe. After scoring our free cookies, I take Vanessa to the playroom where I help her cut out pictures of castles and dragons. Then I draw a picture of a bald princess wearing a sparkling crown, kicking a flaming soccer ball. I punch a hole in each picture and hang them from her IV pole with pink ribbons. Soon our table is surrounded by other kids asking me to create decorations for their poles, too. Before the chemo sucks all my energy for the day I draw unicorns, trucks, flowers, machine guns, and a porcupine. These kids are totally cool. They don't even care that they have cancer. They are sitting here laughing and coloring anyway. It really feels good to draw for them.

Later, I'm back in bed and Mom comes in with a present for me. I know right away what it is—a new cell phone! "Guess who called?!" Mom says after I unwrap it.

"Lizette? Is she home?"

"No, not yet, but I think she sent you a text message."

I flip it open and read.

Iz, so sorry u r sic. OMG there's a TB counselor here. I took a cool drawing class. Great horses here. BFF Liz.

"That's it?! 'So sorry you're sick'?!" I yell. "Like I

just have the flu or something! Then she talks about some stupid counselor." ("TB" is code for Total Babe) Before cancer, I would have actually cared that there was a totally cute counselor, but now it just makes me angry. "Mom, are you sure that's all she wrote?" How could I be here with cancer and my best friend doesn't even care?

"Well, honey, you know they really aren't supposed to have cell phones at the camp."

I ignore Mom and text Lizette back.

I'm not just sick you know. I have cancer.

I want to add "Don't you care?" I want sympathy not a camp newsletter.

OMG r u dying?

Now she's scared. Good.

No. Have to have tons of chemo. Makes me puke. Gotta go. Have to hide phone. Bye L

How convenient. Now she knows I'm not dying so she can go back to her perfect life. I sigh. This is so weird. I'm jealous, but it seems like just ten minutes ago, I was exactly like her. Even though I'm annoyed, I'm really scared that Lizzie won't want to be friends any more. Cancer was stealing everything else in my life, it may as well steal her, too. Who could blame her? She'll have healthy friends to hang out with.

"Are you okay?" Mom asked.

I just roll my eyes.

Vanessa asks me to watch a movie with her. It's a stupid movie about a family of polar bears. Between my nausea and Vanessa's constant chatter, I can't concentrate anyway. Man, I wish I were at camp with Lizette.

The next day I only get one more text from Lizette. It's a lame comment about her falling into the lake. Poor baby. I turn my phone off and watched the rest of my hair fall out. Bye-bye, Mohawk. Later Vanessa goes home, and I have the room to myself. Mom and Dad are out. At least now I can be by myself and cry. It's a relief to be alone for a while. I sob into my pillow.

After I cry my way through a box of Kleenex, Alexis comes in and sits down.

"Want a little company?"

"Okay." By now I'm fresh out of tears.

"You know why I became a counselor, Isabel?"

"Why?"

"I watched my little sister get cancer and go bald. We weren't very close before that. I used to think she was a pest. But when I saw her go through all of that something inside of me changed. Ever since then, I knew I wanted to help sick kids."

"Is she still alive?"

"She sure is, and now she has kids of her own."

"Wow. Did all of her hair grow back?"

"It sure did. Now you'd never know she ever lost it."

"How long does it take to grow back?"

"It starts growing back as soon as your chemotherapy treatments are over."

"I guess I'm gonna be an egghead for a while," I sigh. I still have months of treatment left. But now I have a little more hope.

"Now it's official," I say when Mom and Dad come in. "The Soccer Princess is now the Bald-headed Princess."

"You are so amazing and brave," Mom says, squeezing my hand.

"Don't overdo it, Mom," I say even though I'm loving every word she says.

"Hey kiddo, I got something for you." Dad smiles and hands me a black cap with fuchsia flames on it and "Princess" in sparkly silver letters. On the bill there are tiny little soccer balls studded with rhinestones.

"This is cool. Where did you get it?"

"Oh, let's just say a little fairy from the team made it for you," Dad says slyly. "Just think of it as your official Soccer Princess crown."

"Ha! I can't wait to wear it to the first game in the fall." I'm not sure, but I think I see tears in my dad's eyes.

Later, I turn my phone back on and text Liz.

I'm bald now.

When I don't hear back, I figure it is one of two things. Either they caught her with the cell phone and took it away, or she just doesn't want to be friends with me anymore.

Chapter 10

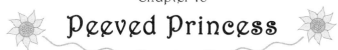 Peeved Princess

This time when I go home, I have to face the world bald. Mom tells me that they are going to get me a wig, but I have mixed feelings about wearing one. She says that she has saved my hair that Shania cut and they could probably make a wig from that, but to me it seems kind of prissy and weird. For now, I think I'll just wear my princess cap.

I have to get through the usual days of low counts and feeling pukey. Like Natalie said, getting chemo is a lot like having a regularly scheduled appointment with the flu. You walk into the hospital knowing that the medicine they're going to give you is most likely going to make you sick as a dog, but you go anyway. Your only other option is death. It's that simple. And after each treatment, you go home waiting for your counts to bottom out, and you get weaker every day. Finally, they rise again and you gradually start feeling better. Then there are a few days, maybe a week if you're lucky, when you feel like your old self and do stuff like everything is normal again. I think about going to high school, maybe even playing soccer in college, me and Lizette getting jobs. I've never really thought about that stuff before, but I guess it's because I always just thought it would be there.

So today I'm feeling really good, and Dad and I go to the park down the street to kick the ball around. "Dad, do you think I'll make varsity when I'm in high school?" I ask.

"Are you kidding, Soccer Princess? You're already one of the best players in the league, and you're the youngest in your division. You'll probably get a college scholarship, go pro, sign a contract with Nike, and buy your old mom and dad a palace."

"And what color would you like your matching Porsches to be?" I grin.

"Why, the team colors, green and gold of course. And don't forget my yacht!"

We're kicking the ball back and forth, running a few drills. I wipe the sweat off my brow and toss my princess cap onto a bench. I'm joking about building a pool the size of a soccer field for the palace when I hear some laughter behind me.

Some kids are laughing at me. My stomach becomes one big knot.

"Hey, look at the bald girl." A group of kids, just sitting on the bleachers doing nothing, look at me from the edge of the field.

"Hey, cue ball! Let me see you bounce the ball off your head!" jeers one of the kids.

A girl next to him nudges him, "Tony, cut it out. She might be sick or something." Uh, duh. Ya think?

Dad's face flashes with fury. Dad, please don't embarrass me. Just don't make it worse. He takes a step towards them.

"Dad, let's just go home," I hiss, my cheeks burning. I feel like I'm in one of those dreams when you're standing in front of class and you're supposed to give a report but you don't know anything about it.

"You should be ashamed of yourselves!" Dad screams. "She's got—"

"DAD! Let's go!" I interrupt reaching for my cap on the bench. The last thing I want is their pity. But that Tony kid snatches up my hat just before I can reach it. He tosses it to one of the other kids and they all start running. Dad lunges towards them, but he is farther away than I am. I have never been this angry in my entire life. I have one focus. They're not getting my hat! My lungs burn and I can barely see through the tears in my eyes. Dad is behind me trying to call me off, but there is no stopping me. I have almost caught up to the kid with the hat. I don't care that he is bigger than me. I plan to kick him hard right behind the knee with my cleats and take him out. But he tosses the hat aside and runs off in the opposite direction. Coward. Gasping, I bend over and pick up my hat. I fall to the ground, vomiting.

Dad kneels down beside me and puts his arms around me. "Dad, why?" I cough. "How can people be so mean?"

"I don't know, baby. They're just a bunch of cowardly bullies. Bullies put others down to make themselves seem more important. They're pathetic. But you, on the other hand, are incredible. Are you okay?"

"Yeah."

"Princess, it's a good thing I didn't catch that kid. I had big plans for my foot and his butt."

Dad helps me up and we walk home. "Those kids make me so mad."

"Isabel, you're so special. Take your angry energy and channel it into something positive."

"Dad, I already am. I'm beating cancer."

Chapter 11

Spider Princess

I haven't been able to shake what happened with those mean kids. I've been really obsessed about being bald, almost daring people to say something. At one of my clinic visits, a boy in the elevator is staring at me. I hear his mother whisper something to him about how it's not polite to stare. "What's the matter?" I yell. "Haven't you ever seen anyone have a bad hair day?" The two of them bolt as soon as the door opens.

"Isabel!" Mom scolds.

"Sorry, Mom," I sigh.

"You know, Izzie, your comment was actually pretty clever. But why don't you try saying it with a smile on your face next time?"

Most of time, though, people are really nice. When my counts are up and I can go places, it's kind of fun when people give me free stuff. I've gotten free candy, free movie passes, skate passes, gift certificates, and lots of cards. I'm bad—I rip the cards open and check to see if there's money inside. I'm saving it so I can go to camp with Lizzie next summer. I was really upset when Mom and Dad told me they couldn't afford it this year, but I guess it all worked out for the best, if you can call this "the best," because I would have had to leave anyway.

Dad calls all the free stuff Cancer Perks or CPs for short.

"Princess, you're a VIP because you are beating cancer. All VIPs deserve special perks," Dad explains.

"Then, can I get a raise in my allowance?"

"Are you kidding? You have more money than I do."

My favorite CP so far is when I got box seat tickets to see my favorite pro soccer team play. I got to meet all of the players and they gave me a signed ball. I even got my picture in the newspaper. Of course, Mom followed me around all day, squirting me with hand sanitizer. The worst part was when I had to use a public restroom. She whipped out the Lysol and doused the seat until it was slippery. "Why don't you just make me take a bath in the stuff?" I said.

"Now there's an idea!" Mom responded cheerfully.

The next time I return to the hospital for chemo, I feel a little more like a hero than some bald freak that people stare at. I hear that Natalie is coming in, too, and I'm looking forward to seeing her.

"So guess who's coming tonight?!" Mom says after I settle in my room.

"Yeah, I know. But I thought Natalie wasn't coming until tomorrow." So maybe she's not the only friend I get to see.

"No, I meant Lizette! She got home from camp today and she can't wait to see you. Isn't that great?"

My heart jumps inside my chest. I am excited and terrified at the same time. Will she still want to be my friend? Will she understand when I'm too sick to hang out? Will she think I'm ugly with no hair?

Mom sits down on the bed next to me. "Oh it's okay, honey. She understands about your hair. She's just happy that you're doing okay," she says, stroking my arm. "True friends always stick by you during tough times," she adds.

"Yeah, I guess you're right," I say. "But it'll still be weird. All of the kids in the hospital are used to baldness, but Lizette's probably never seen a bald kid before."

"Well then, you'll have a chance to teach her about what's important in life, won't you? It's what's on the inside that counts. She'll respect your courage."

"Yeah, I guess she will, after she's done staring."

"Oh, come on," Mom laughs. "It'll be fine, you'll see."

Just after dinner, Lizette and her mom appear in the doorway. They have a huge bag of gifts and a bunch of balloons. "Hi," Lizette says shyly, almost as if she's scared to come in.

"Come in, come in!" Mom chirps. "There are enough chairs here. Sit down."

"Hi, Lizzie," I say softly. Suddenly, I feel shy also. She looks so tan and pretty. I'm glad that I have on my hat.

"We brought you some presents." Lizette sets the bag down on my bed. "First open mine. I made this for you at camp." I try to picture what she could have made me. Is it an "I feel sorry for you gift" like the one a neighbor had sent? A pair of too small, ugly green slippers that still had the clearance tag attached.

I unwrap a tie-dyed shirt that has "Izzie" and a soccer player silk-screened on the front. "Sweet!" I start tearing up. "Does that mean we're still best friends?"

"Of course we are." Lizette unzips her sweater to reveal an identical shirt, except hers says "Lizzie" and has a cheerleader on the front. "Mom told me that you wouldn't be able to start school right away so I thought on the first day you come back we could both wear our shirts."

It feels like a huge weight has been lifted off of my shoulders. I leap out of bed and hug Lizette. She has tears in her eyes. "I was so scared that you wouldn't want a best friend with cancer."

"And I was scared you wouldn't want to hang out with me anymore." She smiles and wiped away her tears. I call her a prissy crybaby. Yep, we're back.

The next gift is two cans of Silly String. Before we know it, we are having a Silly String war, laughing and squirting everything in sight. We bounce on the bed, blasting away at each other until the cans are empty. Our moms have to duck for cover. When we are done, the sheets, the bedrails, and even the walls were coated with neon green strands.

I don't even notice that my hat has fallen off. I realize it when, very gently, Lizette picks up a pile of Silly String and places it on top of my head. "Spider Princess!" she giggles.

"Yeah, that's me," I laugh, modeling my new hair.

"You should have seen me when I had a Mohawk!"

Together we open the rest of the gifts. Some of our neighborhood friends and classmates have heard about my cancer and have given Lizette gifts and cards to bring to me. With books, movies, new clothes, and toys piled on the bed, I feel a little bit like it's my birthday.

"Lizzie, this is awesome. When you stopped texting, I didn't know what to think."

"Well, remember that TB counselor I told you about? He wasn't so hot after all. He took my phone away."

We spend the rest of the visit talking, and I tell Lizzie how I'm saving to go with her to camp next summer. It's fun thinking about the next summer, a summer without cancer.

When it's time for Lizette to leave, I'm exhausted. But I'm happy for the first time since I found out I have cancer. The cancer can take away my hair for a while, but it can't take away my best friend.

Chapter 12

School Princess

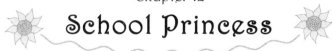

The next day, Chris comes into my room to introduce me to Ms. Fields, the hospital teacher. She extends her hand. "Hi, Isabel. I'm looking forward to working with you."

I shake her hand and look her over. She is a little older than my mom and she's dressed pretty cool. But these days, anyone not wearing scrubs looks cool to me. Ms. Fields has on apple earrings and a button that reads "School: Absence makes the heart grow fonder." That button kind of annoys me. I wonder if she can really make me do work while I'm here.

"School starts next week, and I'll help you keep up while you're here. You'll also have a homebound teacher who'll come to your house when you're at home." She explains how they have a library and wireless laptops at the hospital, but my mind drifts. School's starting! I almost forgot. I won't be there for my first day of sixth grade. I'm moving from elementary to middle school and I won't even be there.

"...and you can access your textbooks online any-time..." Ms Fields is saying. I wonder if Lizette and I will be in the same class. Where will we sit at lunch? Will I make it back before the year's over? Will I still be bald?

I pretend that I have been listening the whole time.

"So, you're like a tutor that helps kids while they're in the hospital."

"That's right." Ms. Field's smiles. "I'll be able to e-mail your regular teachers so I know what you're doing, and I can make sure you're up to speed." So much for lying and telling her I have no homework. "I hear you're pretty smart, so you'll probably make my job easy," she adds.

"But what if I'm too sick to work?"

"That's okay. You can work at your own pace. On the days that you feel well, you'll be able to make up for the bad days. Most of my kids here have no trouble keeping up. I'm sure you'll do fine."

"That's probably true," I agree. "But now that I'm not allowed to go to school, I'll probably miss it."

"What do you like the most about school?"

"My friends. I like it when my best friend, Lizette, and I get to be in the same class. Then we can be work partners. I help her in math and she helps me in English." Then I realize Ms. Fields is asking about school school. "Besides my friends," I say, "That's easy—art. I'm good at drawing."

Then I get a great idea. "Hey! Since you're going to e-mail my teachers, can you see if Lizzie and I can have some of the same classes? That would be awesome if we could do homework and stuff together." If I have to have cancer and do schoolwork, it may as well be as painless as possible.

"Isabel, that's a great idea. I can't make any promises, but I'll see what I can do."

When Ms. Fields leaves, I feel a little less worried about school starting, but I still feel really cheated. I think of all the times I wished that there was no school so I could sleep in. Now I wish that I could go. I'll keep up so I can fit in when I go back. The only thing that's going to look stupid is my hair.

I hear a ball rolling and I look down to see a soccer ball rolling into my room. Then a big foot sticks out from the doorway and kicks it towards my bed. I recognize Chris's size 12 clodhopper. The next thing I know I'm out of bed kicking the ball back, but I forget to unplug my pole so I run out of space like a dog on a leash. "No fair," I laugh.

"C'mon, let's go up on the roof."

So we head up there and kick the ball around a little. "Chris, when your chemo was over, how long did it take for you to be able to play soccer again?"

"Well, let me see. When I finished my high-dose IV chemo, I still had to take some pills that slowed me down a little but only for a little while. I eased back into it, and before I knew it I was going full steam. You'll see. You'll be playing in top form before you know it. And you know, Izzie, you can come to me or Alexis or the psychologists here if you ever need to talk about anything." All of that's a relief.

The next day when Natalie comes in for treatment, I ask her about school. She was diagnosed six months before me, so she had to leave in the middle of the year and then get tutored.

"The work part wasn't that bad," she says. "When you have a teacher all to yourself, the learning goes a lot faster. But I missed my friends. Like last year my friend, Barb, had all of these knock-knock jokes to tease Mrs. Winkler, our math teacher. Pretty soon the whole class started doing it, and it was hilarious. Want to hear one?"

"Yeah! I love jokes."

"Knock, knock."

"Who's there?"

"Hair."

"Hair who?"

"Hair today. Gone tomorrow."

"I love it!" I suddenly have a brilliant idea. "Alexis seems like she can take a joke..."

"Well, I do believe she can." Natalie has a huge smile. "And Ms. Fields might need some work on her sense of humor."

"I believe she does."

"And Chris is always playing, and Freddy and Shania, oh Shania. Do you know what would cheer up all of those people?"

"I believe I do."

"Knock-knock jokes!" we squeal at the same time.

"Okay," Natalie announces, "school's back in session and we have our very first research project—collecting knock-knock jokes."

So we go down to the hospital schoolroom and check out a laptop. Ms. Fields is quite impressed that we

are already working on a project together, but she gives
us a weird look when we tell her it is a secret. Natalie
Googles "knock-knock jokes," and I text Liz and tell her
our mission. She immediately gets on her computer at
home and starts sending some:

Knock knock
Who's there?
Scotta
Scotta who?
Scotta be a funnier joke than this!

Knock knock
Who's there?
Phillip
Phillip who?
Phillip the tank I'm outta gas!

As we giggle, Natalie takes the phone and sends
one to Liz.

Knock knock
Who's there?
Chemo
Chemo who?
Chemo sabe will make you puke!

We get punchy, laughing and reading them to each
other, sending them back and forth with Liz, and writing
them all in a special notebook. I decorate the cover with
a drawing of a woman who looks like Alexis, knocking on
a door to the hospital. Ms. Fields is on the other side
knocking and trying to get out.

When we are ready to road-test our jokes, we find Alexis in the playroom with Josh, Vanessa, and a few other kids. It's perfect.

Natalie begins. "Alexis, how do you manage to hold down such stressful job? I mean, the pressure of being surrounded by kids with cancer and all. You must really need humor in your life." Then we start firing jokes at her. At first Vanessa doesn't get it but once she catches on, she is relentless. We whisper some short ones in her ear and she joins in.

"Knock, knock." Vanessa is jumping up and down in front of Alexis.

"Who's there?"

"Barry."

"Barry who?" Alexis has no choice but to ask.

"Barry the treasure in the back yard!" Vanessa squeals with laughter. Then she continues. "Oh you know what? I had a fish once. I won it at a carnival, but it died. Mommy wasn't too happy because said the food and the bowl and the stones cost more than the stupid thing was worth. I named her Chloe."

"The fish or your mom?" Alexis asks, tears of laughter running down her cheeks.

"Uh, Vanessa, what does your fish have to do with the knock-knock joke?" I ask.

"Because I had to Barry it in the back yard."

The kid is a natural.

Soon the other kids are running up to us to get jokes to tell. We even teach little Josh, who can barely talk, how to say "knock-knock," but when he says it, it comes out "not-not." Pretty soon, he is back tooling around in his little car, saying, "Vroom-vroom, not-not."

Tonight the chemo has me sick on and off, but in between pukes I tell Mom, Dad, and Freddy about our new project. Dad is going to get every soccer player in the league to come up with jokes. As founders of the Stupid Joke Club (SJC), Natalie and I are going to get busy making posters and little mailboxes to deliver jokes to each kid's hospital room. Our motto will be "Beating Cancer One Joke at a Time."

"You'll have a great story to share when you finally do go back to school," Mom says.

"I wonder who my homebound teacher's going to be," I think aloud. "I hope she can take a joke."

Chapter 13
 # Pretty Lucky Princess

The best thing about chemotherapy is that it does a good job killing cancer. The worst thing is that it also does a good job killing the cells inside you that fight off germs. For a kid with cancer, that means a fever is serious business. A cold or an infection that wouldn't mean much to a regular kid could be deadly to someone like me. I suppose that's why this princess's mom is the queen of disinfectant.

Because of the infection risk, while I'm at home, I get my blood counts checked every week, and Mom takes my temperature every day. If it hits 101 degrees, I have to go to the hospital immediately and go on IV antibiotics for several days. This can be really frustrating when you are actually trying to have a life.

So the last week of summer arrives and I'm stuck at home, not allowed to go anywhere or have anyone over. Lizzie calls every day, but it is hard hearing about her swimming and going to the movies or the mall. "Don't worry, Izzie," she says. "When you get better, we'll go on the most amazing shopping spree of all time."

But it seems like I'm not going to get better any time soon. After just a few days at home, I spike a fever and have to head back to the hospital. Mom is really nervous, but Dr. Ruckowski tells her that fevers in chemo patients aren't that unusual. Funny, I'm not nearly as worried as Mom. I'm just annoyed that I have to come back to the hospital so soon.

"You are doing very well," Dr. R assures us. "Next week we'll check your bone marrow to see if you are in remission."

"What if I'm not?" I gasp, joining Mom in the nervous club.

"Then we wait a little while and check it again. Your type of leukemia responds very well to treatment. You'll be fine, Princess." Dr. R smiles gently and his glasses wiggle on the end of his nose. "Most of my kids who have been treated for leukemia are in remission. Some kids with other types of cancer aren't so lucky." Dr. R gets quiet for a second and he looks kind of sad. I wonder who he's talking about. I'm glad it's not me.

When Lizette calls, I tell her a new knock-knock joke.

"Classic, Iz! I didn't know knock-knock jokes could be so funny," she laughs.

"Actually, Natalie and I have started collecting all different types of jokes for our club. Some of the younger kids don't get them. And some others are just sick of knock-knock jokes so—"

"What club?" Lizette interrupts.

Oops, I never told her about the SJC. "Well, Natalie and I started this really cool club." I explain our motto and how we are making little mailboxes for all of the rooms.

"Oh, that's nice, but you never started a club

without me before. Does that mean you don't want to be in the Castle Club any more?"

"Aww, come on, Lizzie. You know I can't go up there right now." She's starting to tick me off.

"Am I allowed to join?" She sounds all whiney like little Ricky.

"Well, it was really just for us kids with cancer, but if you—"

"Fine. You and that Natalie girl can keep your stupid club!"

"You're just jealous because we thought of it first!" I click my phone shut. How can she be so mean? Lizette and I hardly ever fight, but I was fuming. I felt stabbed in the back.

"What's the matter?" Mom said when she came in. "Do you feel sick, honey?"

"Yeah, I'm sick of Lizette." I tell her about our squabble. "Mom, she gets to go to camp, to be a regular kid. How come she's mad at me? I'm the one stuck in the hospital with cancer! It's not fair!"

"Maybe Lizzie's really not mad at you," Mom said. "Maybe she's mad at the cancer. Maybe she's a little jealous of Natalie. And maybe she's afraid she'll lose you. She's always had you all to herself before. Think about how you would feel if she had told you about this great new friend she met at camp." Great. Mathematical Mom always looks at both sides of the equation.

"But Mom, she said our club was stupid," I pout. "She shouldn't have said that."

"Well, it is called the Stupid Joke Club, isn't it?"

I start to smile but I don't want Mom to see me. I wasn't ready to stop feeling sorry for myself. "Whatever," I groan.

So Mom leaves and I decide to go for a walk, just me and my IV pole. A little while back, Natalie and I had decided to name our poles. We figured that if we were going to be stuck with them 24-7, they may as well have names. Mine is Penelope Pole and she has a purple a wig and sunglasses. She lets me brush her hair. She is a good listener.

"Penelope, why couldn't Lizette be happy that I have something to do while I'm here? Why did she have to go and be all snippy like that?" Penelope doesn't answer. Her pump gurgles. She is thinking. "Stupid Liz," I sigh.

I'm so lost in thought and kind of spacing out that I almost walk right into Josh's mom. "Oh hi. How's Josh?" I hope she didn't see me talking to my pole.

"He's not doing so well." She speaks softly and hangs her head. Her eyes are swollen and red. She shuffles away before I can say anything else. I remember what Dr. R had said about some kids' cancers being harder to cure. I walk by the nurses' station. One of the nurses has her arm around Josh's mom. Everyone speaks in whispers and the air feels all heavy and sad.

Later that evening, Josh dies. I think it's Alexis who tells me, but it's like I already know.

"Why? Why did he die?" I cry as Mom holds my hand and Dad sits beside me.

"No one knows why, Princess. Life isn't fair. But I do know one thing. You are not going to die." Dad squeezes my other hand and looks gently into my eyes.

"When I have kids, I'm going to name my first baby Josh."

"Then I sure hope he's a boy," Dad says, smiling with tears in his eyes.

That night I dream that Josh has a head full of curly hair and he is playing on the most amazing playground ever created. It has dozens of toy cars, sparkling rides, a rainbow slide, and tame animals of every species walking around. He smiles at me and waves. "Bye-bye, not-not." When I wake up I am smiling, crying, and waving at the ceiling. My argument with Lizzie seems so silly now. I'm pretty lucky to be alive.

Chapter 14
Princess in Waiting

One more week and they are going to test my bone marrow to see if I am in remission. The antibiotics clear up my infection, so I go home to wait. I'm waiting to see if Liz will call. Waiting to see if the chemo has killed all of the cancer in my body. Waiting sucks.

Meanwhile, everyone else is heading back to school. I'm going to miss all of the excitement of seeing who is in my class, checking out everyone's new clothes, and seeing if any of the dorky boys got cute over the summer. I've always loved organizing all of my stuff in the desk. And I really love the smell of new textbooks. I remember how Ronnie Stein laughed at me on the first day of school last year because he caught me sniffing my social studies book. "But it's so nice and new!" I defended myself. "Try it." Pretty soon everyone at our table group was sniffing their social studies books. When the teacher saw us, she smiled and said that we weren't going to learn anything unless we actually read them. I am going to miss all of it. By the time I get to go, all of the new friends will be made, seats will be filled. All I can do is wait.

At least I'm having a decent week at home. Because my counts are up, Mom says I can go to Nina's birthday party. My cousin's birthday is always the last weekend before school starts, and I usually see friends and relatives that I haven't seen all summer. None of them have seen me bald yet. This is going to be so weird.

"Maybe I shouldn't go," I say to Mom. "You know, germs and all."

"Oh, it's fine, honey. The doctor said your counts are in the normal range right now. It'll be good for you. Besides, Aunt Lucia invited Lizette. Isn't that nice?"

My heart skips a beat. I am still annoyed at Liz. Is she still mad, too?

"I don't know. I'll feel weird going to a party looking like this."

"Hey, Soccer Princess," Dad chimes in. "You didn't get to be first string by running from the ball. Go out there and show them how tough you are. I bet you'll have a blast. Tell them some of your knock-knock jokes."

Aunt Lucia's parties are always huge. She does everything just right with homemade tortillas, arroz con pollo, colorful lanterns, and a huge piñata. Sometimes the adults dance and my Great-uncle Enrique brings out his marionettes to entertain the younger kids. I decide to go and when we get there, the party is already rolling.

I am mobbed by well-wishers and I feel a little like a celebrity. "Nuestra princesa brava," Aunt Lucia proclaims as she squeezes my cheeks. Nina rescues me and drags me out in to the back yard. "C'mon, let's go on my new water slide!" I peel off the cover-up over my bathing suit. Mom stops me and smears my back with sun block. Soon I am slipping down a giant slide and running through sprinklers. We blast each other with water cannons and slosh in the wet grass. When the other kids realize that I won't break or faint, they start treating me like the same old Isabel. It is a great day. Only one more thing would make it perfect. I look around for Lizette but she's not here.

So I busy myself squirting anyone who gets in my way and throwing water balloons at anyone who comes near me. Laughing, I chase Ricky with one and I cock my arm back and let it sail through the air, hoping to nail him in the head. But I miss and it explodes all over some girl's back. She hasn't changed into a bathing suit yet so I go up to her to apologize. Then she turns around and I realize it's Lizette.

For a moment I just stand there, dripping and embarrassed. "Oh, Liz, I'm so sorry. I wasn't aiming for you at all."

Liz shrugs. "That's okay. I don't care about this old outfit anyway."

I laugh. "I know how you feel. I'm having a really bad hair day!"

We giggle and everything feels normal again. After we dry off, Nina, Liz, and I go upstairs to Nina's room. Lizette has brought her make-up case and some fashion mags. She spreads them out on Nina's bed and opens to a page with some short-haired models. "Look at that gorgeous make-up." She points to a glammed-up model with a close-cropped short cut. "Izzie, I can make you look like that. How about it?"

"Well," I hesitate. "I think you should do the birthday girl first." I nod towards Nina. All of our lives, Lizette has been the frilly one. I have never been into make-up like she is. When I try to wear it I, always end up looking like a clown. I watch her as she does Nina, and when she is done, I have to admit she did a good job.

So I let Lizzie do her magic, and for the first time in a long while, I actually feel pretty. "You have great cheekbones," Lizette comments when we are done. The three of us primp in front of the mirror and flip through the magazines. With my makeover and my sparkly cap on, I feel so glam and almost forget I'm sick. I am ready for middle school, even though my cancer isn't.

I glance out the window onto the lawn below and spot a little boy. He looks like Josh. What will happen to me if I don't get into remission?

I try to shrug off my scary thoughts and to surround myself with positive energy like Mom taught me. But the thoughts stay in the back of my mind, and I know that only one thing can chase them away forever.

Chapter 15

Remission Princess

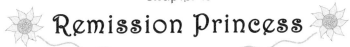

T-Day is here. The way to find out if a leukemia patient is in remission is to test the bone marrow. That's the little blood cell factory inside of our bones. If the new cells are healthy with no sign of cancer, then I'm in remission. If not, well, it means the chemo didn't work. That means that the doctors would have to try something else. Something else really means something worse. Not once have I ever heard a doctor say to anyone in the hospital, "Oh, you're not in remission. Let's try less chemo." Yes, this is the biggest test of my life and there isn't anything I can do to get ready for it.

When the time comes, they put me in la-la land to take the bone marrow sample. I'm pretty groggy, but I remember telling Mom and Dad that I wished I had studied for my blood test. Dad laughed. Mom just paced back and forth. The next thing I know, I am back in my hospital room waiting for the results. Dad is trying to distract us with knock-knock jokes, but Mom gets aggravated. "Rafa, stop it. Can't you be serious for once?"

"I'm just trying to pass the time, honey."

I can tell by the look on Mom's face that Dad would be much better off shutting up. I feel guilty. I know I haven't done anything wrong, but I still feel bad.

"Why don't you just go get us a cup of coffee until Dr. R comes by?" Mom sighs.

"Yes, dear." Dad winks and kisses me on the head. Mom shoots him a look as he scoots out the door.

I'm so relieved when Natalie comes into the room. "Hey, guess what? I'm in my last chemo cycle. Pretty soon I'll be able to blow this Popsicle stand." She pats her IV pole. "Isn't that right, Flo?" Flo wears silk streamers with CDs hanging from them.

I wonder when I'll get to say that I am in my last chemo cycle. I am majorly jealous of Natalie. And I don't want her to stop coming to the hospital.

"But Flo can't leave Penelope," I protest. "They're best friends."

"Oh, yes she can," smiles Natalie. "But she promises to visit."

"But who will tell Penelope dumb jokes?" I am whining now. This place is really going to suck without Natalie.

"Yeah right. You're not going to visit." I snatch my drawing pad off the bedside tray and start sketching furiously. It's not fair. She's almost done. I have months left. And I might not even be in remission. What am I going to do if I'm not in remission? I'm drawing a nasty fire-breathing dragon with claws like daggers. I ignore everyone and keep drawing. Finally, Mom whispers something in Natalie's ear and she leaves. Yeah, you leave, Miss I'm-going-to-blow-this-Popsicle-stand.

Then I hate myself for acting that way. For the

second time in less than a half hour, I feel guilty.

"Princess, you'll be in remission. I just know it. Why don't we watch a movie and let our minds take a little vacation?" Mom suggests. Dad agrees from the doorway, a cup of coffee in each hand.

Mom pulls out one of our family favorites, but I can't concentrate so I keep sketching. Pretty soon, the dragon is surrounded by knights and women warriors with Mohawks. They're heaving spears, needles, and lightning bolts at him. I am lost in my drawing, fighting for remission with my pencil.

So I don't see Natalie come back in until I hear her voice. "Will so." She's standing by my bed with her arms folded across her chest.

"Huh?"

"I will so come see you, dork. You promised to teach me some soccer moves, remember? I plan on practicing in the hallway with you so we can annoy Shania."

For the first time today I smile. "I know you will."

"Oh, guess what?" Natalie continues. "My neighbor owns a craft store and they are donating all of the stuff we need to make decorated mail boxes for our Stupid Joke Club. You know this could be really big."

"Cool."

"Hey," Mom chimes in. "I could help you girls build a Stupid Joke Club website. What do you think?"

Now I'm getting excited. "Yeah! We could send jokes to kids in hospitals all over the country!"

"The world," Natalie adds.

Then I realize two things. First, I have actually forgotten about how scared I am, and second, I absolutely have to be in remission because I have so much to do.

So when Dr. Ruckowski comes into my room with a big smile on his face, we are all ready for the good news. "I have some wonderful news, Princess. You're in remission!"

Mom and Dad hug me with tears in their eyes. Then Mom grabs her phone to call Aunt Lucia.

"Awesome!" I holler, lifting my hands in the air like I just scored a goal. "Does that mean I can blow this Popsicle stand now and go back to school?"

"Well, no, not yet," Dr. R smiles. "You have to keep coming to the hospital for a while so you can get the chemo that will keep you in remission."

"But now we know that the medicine is working!" Dad says.

Now I can picture myself playing soccer again. I can see Lizzie and me redecorating the Castle Club. I imagine Natalie and me delivering our jokes to all the kids still stuck in the hospital after we're cured. I can see my hair growing back and people never even knowing that my lovely locks had temporarily skipped town. Being bald isn't so bad when you know that the cancer is all gone.

Ms. Fields stops by to congratulate me and bring more good news. "It's all arranged. You and Lizette will be in the same homeroom when you go back to school. When your schedule's done, you'll be in some of the same classes, too. And you know what that means?"

"What?"

"School's starting. It's time to get to work."

"Ms. Fields," Natalie pipes up. "I think Isabel's first assignment should be an in-depth study on the history of knock-knock jokes." We all laugh.

"Knock, knock," I begin.

"Who's there?" Ms. Fields gives me a sly look.

"Interrupting cow."

"Interrupting c—"

"MOOOOOOOOOOOO!"

"Oh my, this is going to be quite a learning experience, isn't it?" Ms. Fields eyes twinkle.

And it already is. Becoming the Bald-headed Princess has taught me many things. I have learned that a lot of people love me. I have learned that cancer does not equal death. I have learned not to sweat the small stuff. Dad says there are still lots of adults who haven't learned that lesson, so I'm way ahead of the game. He should know. When he comes back later, he brings a boombox into my room and makes me and Penelope dance the very first remission dance with him.

Oh, I almost forgot one more thing I have learned, probably the most important thing of all. Now that I know all of this stuff, I can't keep it all to myself. When I tell Alexis and Chris the good news about my remission, they decide to throw a remission party for me in the playroom. I make a huge poster that says "I'm in remission. You're next". Natalie and I draw silly faces on balloons and pass them out to the younger kids. We use the party to officially launch the Stupid Joke Club and we hand out little slips of paper with jokes on them.

Later that night Freddy approaches me. "Hey, Izzie. There's a new girl on the floor that was just diagnosed. She's about your age and she's really scared. Do you want to meet her? She might need a bad influence."

"Of course!" I say. "She needs someone to score her a cookie or two. I might even ask her to join the Stupid Joke Club."

Freddy brings me over to her room. "Hi, I'm Isabel. People always used to call me the Soccer Princess, but these days I'm the Bald-headed Princess. Would you like to take the rolling tour?"

Ðear Reader

The idea for *The Bald-Headed Princess* and our heroine Isabel came from my experiences as the mother of a little boy named Christopher who had leukemia. During the four years of his cancer treatments, Chris taught me a lot. I learned about fear, the boredom of the hospital, hope, and the importance of family, not to mention all about the yucky parts of cancer treatment. I learned about incredible bravery and unstoppable humor on the part of my son and all of the young cancer patients that I met.

A few years later, one of the students at the elementary school where I teach was diagnosed with cancer. And I learned that there were no books about cancer for kids his age. I knew that I had to do something. I wanted to take all these experiences and what I learned from Chris and weave it into a cancer story especially for kids.

So, I'm glad I got to introduce you to Isabel. Many of her adventures are based on actual events. Like Isabel, Chris played soccer and worried at first that one of his favorite things to do would be taken away from him. We learned that cancer didn't change who he was, it just slowed him down from time to time. Like Isabel, Chris was teased by his classmates for being bald. I wanted to dash over to the school and scream at all of them like Isabel's dad. But Chris knew better. He told me that he would handle it. He showed them that he was still a regular kid who enjoyed building Legos and telling corny jokes. And like Isabel, Chris had a best friend who stuck by him. We all learned that the best gift you can ever give someone whether they are sick or not is your friendship.

If you are a young cancer patient reading this book, I wish that this story lifts your spirits and brings you hope. If you are reading this book because you know a kid with cancer, don't be afraid to talk and play and laugh or even cry with her. That's what friends are for.

If you (or your parents) want to find out more about cancer or cancer treatment, check out
- the Leukemia and Lymphoma Society
   (www.leukemialymphoma.org),
- the Children's Cancer Association
   (www.childrenscancerassociation.org),
- the National Children's Cancer Society
   (www.nationalchildrenscancersociety.com),
- and the American Cancer Society
   (www.cancer.org).

These organizations offer lots of support and good information.

I hope you enjoyed Isabel's story. Hang tough and as Chris always used to say, don't spoil the magic.

Your friend,

Maribeth Ditmars